To
Gabriella ♡
Believe in Yourself Always!
Natalie Lynn Smith ♡

To DJ Montague Elementary School
~My students~
Thank you for all your inspiration!
Love,
Mrs. Smith

MASCOT® BOOKS

www.mascotbooks.com

A Stranger in the Clearing

For more information, please contact:
Mascot Books
620 Herndon Parkway, Suite 320
Herndon, VA 20170
info@mascotbooks.com

Library of Congress Control Number: 2019919603

CPSIA Code: PRTWP0720A
ISBN-13: 978-1-64543-022-3

Printed in South Korea

A STRANGER
IN THE CLEARING

Written by
Vikki Lynn Smith

Illustrated by
Marcela Werkema

Leaves rustled as the evening breeze blew high across the treetops in the Woods. Overhead, clouds formed creatures of gray and white as the sun set slowly past the horizon. The Woods were quiet while the animals waited patiently for a safe hour to venture from their hiding places. Tiny, one of the Cotton Tail brood, came scampering across a fallen log, a golden retriever on his tail.

"Hey, Sequoia!" hollered Mr. Fox.
"Leave that baby alone! You know better than to chase a rabbit! Don't you have anything better to do?"

Sequoia stopped in her tracks and turned toward the fox in a flash. "Why, howdy, Mr. Fox!" she barked. "I didn't see you crouching there. I was just having some fun with Tiny." Sequoia smiled brightly. "You know I wouldn't hurt a fly."

Mr. Fox stood to greet his old friend
who lived among the humans. Then
he turned to the giggling rabbit and
asked, "Is that right, Tiny?"

"That's right!" said Tiny, smiling. "But
I'm not a fly!"

"Will you be going to the meeting in the Clearing tonight, Sequoia?" Mr. Fox asked. "Mrs. Finch and her two young'ins, Tattle and Merry, told me about it and I reckon they'll be there."

"We will indeed," said Mrs. Finch as she swooped in with her family. "That is if Tattle and Merry can stop squabbling over berries all day!"

Sequoia laughed at the bickering baby birds. "I might be able to sneak over to the Clearing while my family is eating dinner. I usually play with my toys outside then."

"I'll be there, of course," replied Mr. Fox. "I always like to find out what's new in the Woods."

Sequoia peered through the trees toward her house. "I'd better get back before my mom comes looking for me. Hope to see everyone at the meeting!"

But that night Sequoia found herself stuck inside, nose pressed against the window, while her family was out at the movies. *So much for the meeting*, she thought.

Sequoia watched outside for
any sign of the backyard animals'
return. Even Sequoia's friends, the
Graysquirrel family, had gone to the
meeting. It was quiet. Nothing stirred
except some frogs in a nearby pond.

Sequoia resigned herself to her down-filled bed.
She'd have to watch the Animal Adventure
station on the family's television for the rest
of the night. Sequoia smiled to herself; living
with humans did have its perks.

Suddenly, Sequoia saw the Graysquirrel
family arrive at their tree. She let out a belly
bark, trying to get their attention, but it was
no use. The family merely scurried up their
tree and nestled into their nest. Sequoia
would have to wait until tomorrow to
hear all about the meeting.

Early the next morning as the sun peeked through the trees, the Woods awoke. Sequoia loved this time of day. After her mom let her out of the house, she ran to the Woods, pretending she was wild, roaming the grounds and smelling all the new smells. As she came upon the Clearing, Sequoia slowed her run to a bouncing trot.

"I wonder what they talked about out here last night," she said to no one in particular.

"They talked about me," came a small voice, hidden behind a thick bush on the outskirts of the Clearing.

"Who's there?" Sequoia inquired, stopping in her tracks to look at the talking bush as it wiggled and shook. Suddenly, the sunlight above shone down upon the Clearing in front of the greenery, exposing the most beautiful creature Sequoia had ever seen.

"My name's Pi. Who and...what are you?"

Sequoia stood still, holding her tail upright, too afraid to speak. "I...uh... I'm Sequoia, a golden retriever dog," she whispered. "What are you?"

"I'm a deer," said Pi sadly. "A Piebald Deer."

"A what deer?" Sequoia asked. "I have lots of deer friends and you don't look like any of them."

The sunlight lifted off the creature's brown speckled back and now its white body looked even more magnificent. Tears formed in the small deer's brown eyes as she whispered, "I am special. I was born this way and no one is like me." More tears began to fall. "I don't fit in...and the other deer don't like me."

"Why don't they like you?" asked Sequoia in her friendliest voice.

"When I'm with the other deer, humans can see me from afar and they come to hunt us. My family must keep me covered all the time, and I'm not allowed to go out into the fields to eat or play. My legs are short so I can't run or jump like the other deer." The little deer took a big breath. "I didn't want to be a burden anymore, so I ran away."

With tears still streaming down her cheeks, Pi threw herself to the bed of the woods and began to cry harder.

Pi's crying drew the attention of the nearby animals of the Woods. They had heard her story at the meeting in the Clearing and they felt sorry for the small white creature. Grey Squirrel and Tiny moved in closer to the animals, hoping to hear them better, while Tattle Finch and Merry Finch soared down to a lower branch to listen in too. They couldn't wait to hear what the dog of the human world would say to this outcast of the Forest.

"Don't cry," said Sequoia softly. "You're here now. I'm sure my friends can help you."

Pi shook her head. "I told King Deer and all the animals last night about why I left my family and the Great Forest!"

"What did they say?" Sequoia couldn't imagine leaving her family.

"They said I need to go home!" Pi heaved her chest as tears began to fall faster down her face. "I didn't want to run away again, so I hid in this bush all night."

Sequoia spoke gently to the white deer. "Oh Pi! Please don't cry. I'm sure that's not what King Deer meant at all. Why, the animals in the Woods are the nicest animals in the whole world. The animals I know would love you for yourself. You wouldn't have to hide in bushes or keep from playing games if you stayed here. When I first came to the Woods, they were scared of me, but I came every day to show them how friendly I was. Now, even the baby rabbits love to play with me!"

"But King Deer told me I had to go home last night!" cried Pi.

"You must have heard him wrong," replied Sequoia, shaking her head.

"No, Sequoia," came a kingly voice. "She did not hear wrong." King Deer stepped out into the Clearing. "But I'm afraid we were wrong. Allow me to explain."

King Deer's strong legs stomped the ground as he moved closer to the smaller deer. "We knew your family must be worried, so we thought if we told you that you couldn't stay, you would return to them. But we didn't truly understand the danger you were in and the sacrifice you had made for them. Once we realized it, I searched for your family in the Great Forest all night. When I found them, I told them you were safe and asked them to join us too. There are no hunters in these Woods. All will be safe here."

Pi's brown eyes brightened as she took in the information from the large buck before her.

"My dear Pi," he continued, "you are the most prized deer in the Woods, not because of the way you look but because **you are YOU**. You are caring and kind, thinking of others before yourself. You risked your life when you left the Great Forest to protect the deer that are hunted there. You even gave up the family you love to keep them safe. Little Pi, it's your actions that make you special."

Sequoia let out a bark of joy. "I told you my friends would love you for yourself!"

Pi's crying turned to a smile as she faced the nearby animals. "Are you sure you don't mind me and my family staying here with you?"

The animals smiled and began to speak and cheer as they circled the special Piebald Deer. They began to chant a song just as special as their new friend...

Piebald, Piebald, white as white,

No more worries, no more fright.

Stay with us in our special woods,

And be a part of our neighborhood!

And so it was on that day, the animals sang and laughed and
played. They all gave thanks to their new friend, for showing them
courage without end.

DID YOU KNOW...

Scientific Name: Odocoileus virginianus

Nickname: Piebald

Diet: Herbivore

Lifespan: Most live into adulthood

Size: 1 – 3.9 feet at the shoulder (Piebald, genetic mutation)

Location: Across the world where white-tailed deer are present

Best Known For: Its unique genetic mutation (changes that do not fit the definition of a white-tailed deer). There is LESS than 1 out of 100 chance of being mostly white.

The Piebald Deer is a rare white-tailed deer found throughout the world where deer breed. The Piebald Deer gets its name from Pie, meaning "mixed up" and bald, or "having a white spot." Its coat can vary from a pinto pony-looking coat of equal patches of white and brown all the way to pure white with few brown patches.

The Piebald population is less then two percent of the white-tailed deer population. The Piebald can grow to the normal heights of other white-tailed deer (from 1 – 3.9 feet at its shoulder) but the Piebald Deer tends to have shorter legs, a curvier back, a roman nose, and on rare occasions, a different eye color than the white-tailed deer.

Many Piebald Deer do not live long due to illness, scoliosis, arthritis, and other ailments not normally found within deer populations. The Piebald Deer is easily spotted by hunters, which make it an easy prey. The Piebald Deer is not an Albino deer (meaning all white).

Interesting Fact: The Bald Eagle is part of the Piebald family.

For more information, activities, and lesson plans, go to VikkiLynnSmith.com

REFERENCES

https://en.wikipedia.org/wiki/Piebald

https://www.qdma.com/look-inside-piebald-deer/

https://www.wideopenspaces.com/10-beautiful-piebald-whitetail-deer-pictures-pics/

https://www.nationalgeographic.com/animals/mammals/w/white-tailed-deer/

ABOUT THE AUTHOR

Vikki Lynn Smith's love for writing began when she was very young as she chronicled living and traveling around the world. She has climbed the Washington Monument, lunched at a Paris café, hiked the forests of Germany, and rode the waves of Hawaii. Through it all, her love for writing grew. As a retired teacher, Vikki began writing stories to inspire her students and from there, a series of stories was brought to life. After years of creating stories, she is thrilled to share her adventures and love for animals in her first book series, In the Woods. When she is not writing, Vikki spends time with her husband, two grown children, and (of course) her two loving Golden Retrievers on the shores of Virginia. To Vikki Lynn Smith, there is no adventure too big or too small that can't inspire the mind to write!

For more information visit: VikkiLynnSmith.com

I'd like to thank my many students who inspired this story. Your illustrations and critiques were priceless. To my family, thank you for your continued support and technical advice in making my dreams come true.

ABOUT THE ILLUSTRATOR

Marcela Werkema is a Brazilian animator and illustrator who has been producing content for children's books for several years. She received her BA in Animation from the Federal University of Minas Gerais (UFMG) and she is now living in Itajaí, a coastal city in the southern region of Brazil. She is the creative director on an animated series and also works as illustrator on many different projects.

www.marcelawerkema.com